W9-BFM-151

Dear Parent:
Your child's love of reading starts here!

Every child learns to read in a different way and at his or her own speed. Some go back and forth between reading levels and read favorite books again and again. Others read through each level in order. You can help your young reader improve and become more confident by encouraging his or her own interests and abilities. From books your child reads with you to the first books he or she reads alone, there are I Can Read Books for every stage of reading:

SHARED READING
Basic language, word repetition, and whimsical illustrations, ideal for sharing with your emergent reader

BEGINNING READING
Short sentences, familiar words, and simple concepts for children eager to read on their own

READING WITH HELP
Engaging stories, longer sentences, and language play for developing readers

READING ALONE
Complex plots, challenging vocabulary, and high-interest topics for the independent reader

I Can Read Books have introduced children to the joy of reading since 1957. Featuring award-winning authors and illustrators and a fabulous cast of beloved characters, I Can Read Books set the standard for beginning readers.

A lifetime of discovery begins with the magical words "I Can Read!"

Visit www.icanread.com for information
on enriching your child's reading experience.

I Can Read® and I Can Read Book® are trademarks of HarperCollins Publishers.

Fancy Nancy: Toodle-oo, Miss Moo

ISBN 978-0-06-288870-9 (trade bdg.) —ISBN 978-0-06-284389-0 (pbk.)

Book design by Brenda E. Angelilli and Scott Petrower

19 20 21 22 23 LSCC 10 9 8 7 6 5 4 3 2 1 ❖ First Edition

Disney Junior

Fancy NANCY

Toodle-oo,
Miss Moo

Adapted by Victoria Saxon
Based on the episode
by Andy Guerdat

Illustrations by the
Disney Storybook
Art Team

HARPER
An Imprint of HarperCollinsPublishers

My family is selling our things
that we no longer need or want
at the Clancy Family Yard Sale!

Ooh la la!

Yard sales are fun.

5

My family doesn't make a lot
of money, but we have fun.
Dad is very good at making deals.

6

I set up my old things

at my own fashion *boutique*.

That's French for a fancy store.

"Nancy, is there anything in here you want to keep?" asks Mom.

"These are baby things," I tell her.

"Why would I want to keep them?"

"Why are you selling your stuff?"
my little sister, JoJo, asks.
"Getting rid of old things
is part of growing up," I say.

Then I see Miss Moo.

I got her for my third birthday.

She was my favorite toy.

"It's been forever since

I've seen you, Miss Moo," I say.

"Remember when we first met?"

Miss Moo is just a baby toy,

but I adore her!

She makes different animal sounds

when you push her buttons.

Bree's little brother, Freddy,

sees Miss Moo.

"I really, really want it," he says.

I don't want to sell her.

I want to keep her forever!

"Miss Moo is not my best toy

for sale," I tell Freddy.

"Sorry," I whisper to Miss Moo,

"I only said that

because I can't give you up."

I try to hide Miss Moo,

so nobody can buy her.

I really want to keep her.

15

But Frenchy finds Miss Moo.

Dad picks her up and takes her

back to the yard sale.

Freddy sees Miss Moo again.

"There it is!" he says.

He runs home to get his mom

so she can buy Miss Moo for him.

Bree wants to surprise Freddy
with Miss Moo for his birthday.
She buys her from Dad.

"Look what I got Freddy," Bree says.

She holds up Miss Moo.

"He is going to love this."

I am more than sad. I'm devastated.

I must get Miss Moo back from Bree.

I catch up with Bree.

"May I have Miss Moo back?" I ask.

"*S'il vous plaît?*"

That's French for please.

"But why?" Bree asks me.

I don't know what to say.

I tell Bree I've already promised

Miss Moo to a mystery customer who

loves her as much as she loves Paris.

21

Bree smiles.

She understands that I am

the mystery customer.

"Don't feel bad," Bree says.

"I still have baby toys too."

"No one understands me

like you," I tell her.

"Best friends, you and me,"

I start our chant.

"Better friends there could not be,"

we say at the same time.

We go back to the yard sale.

"Now I have to find Freddy
another birthday present,"
says Bree.
"It's his third birthday."
I remember my third birthday.

Here comes Freddy with his mom.

"It's a cow who makes

animal noises!" he tells her.

"Sounds like quite a toy," she says.

"Birthdays are important

when you are three," I say.

Freddy needs Miss Moo.

Bree and I agree.

Bree gives Miss Moo to Freddy.

"From me and Nancy," Bree says.

Freddy is really happy.

"Thank you!" Freddy says.

"It's my pleasure, Freddy," I say.

"Toodle-oo, Miss Moo."

Fancy Nancy's Fancy Words

These are the fancy words in this book:

Ooh la la—French for wow

Boutique—French for a fancy store

Devastated—more than sad

S'il vous plaît—French for please